Word List

Here is a list of words that might make it easier
to read this book. You'll find them in boldface
the first time they appear in the story.

Angelo	AN-juh-loh
Venice, Italy	VE-nuhs, I-tuhl-ee
gondola	GON-doh-luh
canals	kuh-NALS
Modesto	MOH-des-toh
Italian	uh-TAL-yuhn
American	uh-MAIR-uh-kuhn
Chicago	shuh-KO-goh
European	YER-uh-pee-uhn
masquerade	mas-kuh-RAYD
sapphires	SA-feyers
zaffiri	zof-FEE-ree
pigeons	PI-juhns
mansion	MAN-shun
sequins	SEE-kwuhns
Duchess Venezia	DUH-chus ven-ET-zee-uh
Arrivederci	uh-ree-vuh-DAIR-chee
gelato	je-LO-toh
receipt	ri-SEET
signature	SIG-nuh-cher
harlequins	HAR-li-kwuhns

Barbie™

Secret of the Three Teardrops

BARBIE and associated trademarks are owned by and used under
license from Mattel, Inc. © 1999 Mattel, Inc. All Rights Reserved.
Published by Grolier Books, a division of Grolier Enterprises, Inc.
Story by Jacqueline A. Ball. Photo crew: Tom Wolfson, Susan Kurtz, Susan Cracraft,
Tim Geison, Dave Bateman, Patrick Kittel, Vince Okada, and Lisa Collins.
Produced by Bumpy Slide Books. Scrapbook designed by Riordan Design.
Printed in the United States of America.
ISBN: 0-7172-8961-3

Barbie turned to the well-dressed man sitting next to her. "**Angelo,**" she exclaimed, "it feels like I'm inside a history book or a painting! I can't believe I'm really here in **Venice, Italy!**"

Barbie felt as though she had entered a magical city. She was riding in a graceful, open boat with one tall, curved end. It was called a **gondola.** It floated through streets of water, called **canals.** Beautiful buildings, which were hundreds of years old, lined both sides of the canals.

Angelo **Modesto** smiled. His dark brown

eyes twinkled behind thick glasses. His face was tan, yet his hair was almost white. He spoke English well, with a thick **Italian** accent. Angelo worked at the Venice City Museum. He was the assistant to the museum's director, Gina Morelli. He had been sent to meet Barbie at the train station.

"Venice is built on 120 islands," he told Barbie. "So we use canals instead of roads. We go everywhere in boat taxis, or in gondolas like this one. I've lived in Venice my whole life. But I never tire of its beauty."

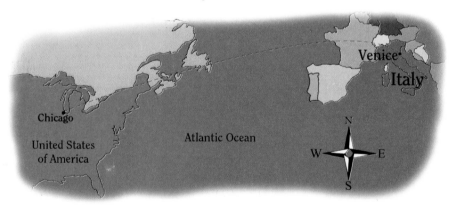

Barbie was the director of the **American** Museum in **Chicago.** She had flown to Italy for a very special reason. For several months now, she had been working on a project with other American and **European** museums. They had worked together to design a special group of ball gowns. All the dresses were copies of gowns worn in Venice centuries ago. Now Barbie was going to take the gowns on a traveling show through Europe and America. Tickets to the show would raise millions of dollars. The money was needed to help restore the art of Venice.

The tour would open that night with a **masquerade** ball at the museum. The guests would wear fancy masks and costumes. Everyone had given money to the project. Barbie would give a speech. All of the gowns would be displayed at the ball. And as a special thank-you, Barbie would get to wear one of the gowns made for the tour.

"You've worked so hard to make this tour happen," said Angelo. "You should be proud!"

"I'm not the only one who's worked hard," Barbie replied. "If we had a dollar for every hour of help given, we wouldn't need the tour. We'd have all the money we need!"

"But then you wouldn't get to travel to Venice," Angelo teased. "Or anywhere else you're going to take those gowns."

"You're right," Barbie agreed. "It was nice of you to meet me at the train station."

"It was my pleasure," Angelo told her. "I mean that. The museum is crazy with plans for the ball tonight. I was glad to escape!"

The gondola approached a dock. A worker on the dock threw a line to the boat.

"Is my hotel nearby?" Barbie asked as she stepped out of the gondola.

"Not far," Angelo answered as he followed her. "But Gina has asked that you come to the museum first, if you don't mind. She wants you to have a final fitting of your ball gown. I will have your suitcases taken to your hotel."

"That's fine, Angelo," said Barbie.

"Besides, I can't wait to see the dress! Not to mention the Three Teardrops."

"Ah, yes. The famous teardrop-shaped **sapphires.** We call them *zaffiri* in Italy," Angelo explained. "The blue gems are the museum's most prized possession. We have guarded them for more than fifty years. If anything ever happened to them, it would be very sad. For Venice, for the museum, and for me."

Barbie paused. Then she added, "To help me get ready for the tour, Gina sent me pictures of the gowns. She explained the story behind each one. But she hasn't told me about the gown that I'll be wearing tonight. Gina said she wants it to be a surprise. But she said it has something to do with the Three Teardrops."

Angelo nodded. "The story of the Three Teardrops is so special to the museum. You must hear it from Gina in person."

"I can hardly wait!" Barbie replied.

Chapter Two

Barbie and Angelo walked through a large outdoor plaza. They paused in front of a giant stone church. Flocks of gray **pigeons** fluttered and swooped. Groups of travelers walked around or sat at little tables drinking coffee.

"There are so many people!" exclaimed Barbie.

"And almost as many pigeons," Angelo joked. "St. Mark's Square is known all over the world as a meeting place. But at high tide, look out. It is sometimes underwater!"

They continued down a twisty lane, away

6

from the square. Interesting small shops lined the street on either side. Their windows held pretty glass objects, fine leather shoes, and beautiful masquerade costumes.

Dazzling masks were everywhere. Some were made to cover the whole face. Others were made to cover only the eyes. Many were decorated with fancy feathers and lace.

"Do you know about Venice's history of masquerade balls?" Angelo asked Barbie.

"Yes," she answered. "That's why Gina suggested we kick off the tour with a masked ball. She said that many years ago, Venice used to hold a big carnival right after Christmas. Everyone dressed up in costumes and wore masks."

Angelo laughed. "It used to last for months. This city sure knows how to throw a party! Now we have a much shorter carnival, in February. But we are still famous for our masked parties."

The two walked up steps leading to a high

stone bridge. Below them was a boat full of sparkling glassware and crisp white tablecloths.

Angelo waved down to the driver. "Those things are being delivered for this evening's ball. Gina will be so pleased. The museum is just across this bridge," he said, pointing.

The Venice City Museum was a pale yellow **mansion** with white trim.

"What a lovely building," Barbie declared. "You're lucky to work here, Angelo."

His smile grew a little smaller. Barbie even thought she saw him frown. "Ah, yes. Lucky," he sighed. "That is why I have stayed here for twenty years, working for many different directors." Then his smile widened again. "But Gina is very able. Even though she is young, she is a strong leader and full of energy."

Angelo held open the heavy wooden door for Barbie. The two entered the museum. Then he led her to an office door. Inside, a short young woman was speaking in Italian on a telephone. She was looking out a window, running her hand through her dark curls. Barbie couldn't understand what she was saying. But Barbie could tell that the woman was upset.

"Gina," Angelo whispered, "our American visitor is here."

Gina turned and saw Barbie. Her face brightened. She spoke briefly into the phone and then hung up.

"Barbie!" exclaimed Gina. "How wonderful to meet you at last. Just wait until you see the gowns! You will be thrilled!" Then she sighed. "But now we have a big problem. Angelo, the tablecloths haven't arrived yet. How are we to have a party without tablecloths? Would you please go see what happened to them?"

"They're right outside," Angelo calmly told her. "The boat just pulled up. I'll go watch the unloading." He made a little bow to Barbie and left.

"What a delightful man," Barbie said to Gina.

"Angelo is a treasure," the director agreed. "He's been here so long, he knows more about the museum than I do! In fact, I used to work for him! I'm lucky he didn't get angry when I was made director instead of him." Gina smiled.

Barbie thought back to the frown that had passed over Angelo's face. But she said nothing.

Gina continued, "And speaking of treasures— come! I simply can't wait another minute to show you the Three Teardrops."

Barbie followed her through marble hallways. Beautiful paintings in bright gold frames hung on every wall. They passed a ballroom set up with tables and chairs and a place for a band.

Around the next corner, they passed a security guard. Then they walked straight into a world of blue.

Blue silk hugged the walls and hung from the windows. Blue velvet carpet covered the floor.

And inside a glass case were the biggest, bluest jewels Barbie had ever seen.

Barbie gasped. "Wow!" she exclaimed.

"They're just beautiful!" The giant sapphires were the deep, clear blue of the ocean on a sunny day. They were wider near the bottom and came to a long, graceful point at the top. "They really do look like teardrops," Barbie said.

"And for good reason," Gina told her, smiling mysteriously. "It's a wonderful story. I'll tell it to you after your fitting," she promised.

Chapter Three

Barbie and Gina went to the workroom for Barbie's fitting. An older woman with blond hair was kneeling beside a dressmaker's dummy. A brown silk gown with a ruffled hem hung on the dummy. The woman was holding several pins in her mouth, stitching the gown.

"This is our seamstress, Toni," Gina said.

Toni waved and nodded at them. But she continued with her work.

"Toni's from the studio in Rome where the gowns were made," Gina explained. "She came to Venice to finish sewing them. Except for your gown, they're all done. The one she's finishing is her own for tonight's ball. She even made costumes for me and Angelo."

Across the room, twenty beautiful ball gowns hung on a long rack. They were in rich, jewel-like colors: ruby, emerald, turquoise. Some were covered with pearls and **sequins.** Others were made of silky fabrics or soft velvet.

Barbie rushed across the room for a closer look. "They're fantastic! They're even more beautiful than in the pictures!"

"Aren't they amazing?" Gina asked. "As you know, they are all copies of gowns worn by rich ladies long ago. In fact, this museum was once the home of **Duchess Venezia.** And she held wonderful masquerade balls here. She was also the original owner of the Three Teardrops."

Barbie looked out through glass doors to a carved stone bench sitting on a brick patio. The surrounding garden was bursting with yellow, blue, and red flowers. She could also see a shovel and a wheelbarrow. They seemed strangely out of place in the lovely garden.

Gina looked over Barbie's shoulder. "The duke and duchess loved to sit out there in the garden," Gina explained. "But the museum has run out of space. Tomorrow work will begin on an addition. It will extend past the bricks outside."

A sudden noise made Barbie and Gina turn around. They saw Toni picking up the scissors and tape measure she had just dropped. The seamstress looked embarrassed. But her lips were still held tightly together.

"I keep telling Toni it's dangerous to hold pins in her mouth," Gina said. "But she says that's how her grandmother taught her to sew. Ready to try on your dress, Barbie?" Gina removed a stunning gown from a small closet.

"Oh, it's gorgeous!" Barbie cried. The dress was a vision in cream, gold, and blue. The front of the skirt was a deep blue satin with a sheer blue overlay. A gold-and-white teardrop pattern covered the rest of the dress. The full sleeves were trimmed in gold. Three tiny, blue bows decorated the front of the gown.

"The bows mark the places where Toni will put the copies of the Three Teardrops," Gina explained. "If they ever get here! We ordered two sets of copies made in case one set got damaged or scratched. I'm glad we did! One set was supposed to be delivered yesterday and one today. But so far, nothing has come."

Suddenly there was a loud knock at the door. Angelo came in, looking worried.

"Excuse me," he began, "but there is an emergency, Gina. The tablecloths are all too big. And there is no time to get others. Also, a

16

photographer is here to take Barbie's picture."

"What?" Gina cried. "That photo shoot was scheduled for tonight, at the ball!"

Angelo looked down at the floor. "She called yesterday with a change of plans," he explained quietly. "With everything going on, I forgot to tell you. The photographer says she won't make her deadline if she doesn't take Barbie's picture now."

"*World Art* magazine is doing a story on our dress tour," Barbie added. "We were counting on the attention to help the show."

Gina looked alarmed. "But we have no sapphires to put on the gown." Then she snapped her fingers. "I know! We can use the real ones! We can stitch them into place."

Angelo gasped. "The real ones? I don't think that is wise, Gina! What if something happens to them?"

Gina sighed. "It's the only thing we can do,

Angelo. We can't lose that magazine photo. And besides, nothing will happen to the jewels. The guard is still on duty. The public has not been allowed in today, so there are no strangers around." She handed him a small key. "Here. Please go get the jewels from the case."

Shaking his head, Angelo took the key and left.

"Sometimes Angelo worries too much," Gina told Barbie. "But those sapphires have been in our safekeeping for many years. I guess I can't blame him." She turned to Toni. "Are you ready for Barbie's fitting?"

Toni stood up and took the pins out of her mouth.

"Of course," she replied, smiling. "I will finish up my gown later. Let me look for some invisible thread to stitch the jewels in place." Barbie watched as Toni began to search through her large sewing basket.

As the seamstress pushed aside a pincushion, something sparkly caught Barbie's eye. "They're probably buttons or sequins for the gowns," she thought.

A few minutes later, Barbie was dressed in the lovely cream-and-blue gown.

Gina pressed her fingertips together and kissed them. "*Bella,* Barbie. You are beautiful!"

"Toni deserves the praise," Barbie corrected. "The dress fits perfectly."

But Toni was frowning. "No. It is too long. You will trip." She knelt down and pinned the hem of the dress. Then, using tiny, expert stitches, she quickly began to shorten it.

"So, Gina, will you tell me the story of the Three Teardrops now?" Barbie begged. "I can't wait to hear it!"

"Oh, yes!" replied Gina.

Just then Angelo returned with the jewels. Toni was snipping off the last hem threads with

small, sharp scissors. Angelo carefully set down the sparkling sapphires on a cabinet.

Toni picked up one of the sapphires. She held it up against the dress.

"Perfect!" Gina cried.

"Gina, the photographer is waiting," Angelo reminded her.

Gina's face showed impatience. "We'll be ready in five minutes, Angelo. We still need to put the gems on the gown."

Angelo looked very upset as he left the room.

Gina settled into a chair. As Toni worked on the dress, Gina told Barbie the story of the Three Teardrops.

"Many years ago, a duke's son fell in love with a smart, beautiful maid. She worked in his parents' house. Her name was Venezia, which is the Italian name for Venice. Her hair was blond, and her eyes were as blue as the sea."

Gina gazed out at the garden. "The young man's family wouldn't let him marry a maid. He suggested that they run away together. But Venezia did not want to come between him and his family. So one day she left.

"The young man was heartbroken. He wandered sadly from room to room. He didn't eat. And soon he did nothing but sleep on the garden bench where they used to sit and talk for hours. Worried about their son, his parents found Venezia and brought her back.

"When Venezia saw her love sleeping on the garden bench, she wept with joy. Seeing how much she loved their son, his parents began to cry, too. Finally the young man awoke. He said that he had been dreaming of a soft spring rain falling on his face. What he had been feeling, of course, were the tears of the three people who loved him so much."

"What a beautiful story!" Barbie sighed.

"His parents blessed their marriage with a gift of three teardrop-shaped sapphires," Gina continued. "Three, to stand for three generations: the parents, the young couple, and their future children. Teardrops, for tears of healing, joy, and family love. And sapphires, to match Venezia's blue eyes. Venezia had the gems sewn into her wedding dress. And you will be wearing a copy of that very dress tonight, Barbie."

Suddenly Toni dropped one of the jewels she had been holding. Everyone swooped down to catch the sapphire at the same time. Barbie caught the gem, and all three women sighed with relief.

But were Barbie's eyes playing tricks on her? She thought she saw very faint marks on the sapphire. Two straight lines, with bars across the top and bottom. "It must be the way the light is hitting the gem," she thought.

Suddenly Angelo burst in again. This time

he was followed by a woman with a camera.

"I am sorry, Gina," Angelo apologized. "The photographer says she cannot wait one more minute. And I still don't know what you want to do with those tablecloths."

Gina looked very annoyed. "All right, Angelo! Toni, you stay with Barbie in case the gown needs adjusting. Angelo, please wait in my office. Toni will tell you when you can put the jewels back. And I will go solve the tablecloth problem!"

Angelo's smile was gone. In its place was an angry, embarrassed scowl.

Chapter Four

After the photo shoot, Toni removed the sapphires from the gown. Barbie went behind a screen to change. When she came out, Toni was handing Angelo the sapphires.

"Once the imitation sapphires arrive, I will sew them on. Then I will send the dress to your hotel," Toni told Barbie. "*Arrivederci!*" she said, waving.

"Good-bye, and thank you," Barbie replied.

Barbie stepped outside the museum. She didn't feel like going to her hotel right away. So she decided to take a stroll and look for some gifts for her sisters.

Barbie bought a small glass cat for Stacie and a necklace for Skipper. She also found a toy gondola for Kelly. Then Barbie stopped for some delicious Italian ice cream, called **gelato.**

In a bookstore, Barbie looked through a book on the history of Venice. She was startled by a painting of a lovely woman with blond hair and blue eyes. Her gown was cream, blue, and gold. It was decorated with three blue jewels.

"It's Duchess Venezia in her wedding dress," thought Barbie. She bent closer to the page. "She reminds me of someone. But I can't think whom."

Barbie peered even more closely. The sapphires in the picture looked much darker than the ones at the museum. But she told herself that a picture in a book could never match the gems' true color.

Using the directions Gina had faxed her, Barbie found her hotel. Up in her room, Barbie's

suitcases were neatly piled in her closet. There was also a long, white bag hanging from the rod, containing her gown.

"The imitation sapphires must have arrived right after I left," Barbie thought.

A smaller bag held a blue, feather-trimmed mask on a stick. It also held a jeweled purse.

"How lovely!" she said out loud.

Just then the phone rang. It was Gina.

"Something terrible has happened!" Gina cried. "I must speak with you. I'm coming right over!"

Fifteen minutes later, Barbie answered the door. The museum director came racing into Barbie's room. Her words spilled out in a rush.

"It's the Three Teardrops!" exclaimed Gina. "They're gone!"

"Gone?!" cried Barbie. "What happened?"

Gina gulped and sat down. "After I settled the tablecloth business, I went back to my office.

On the way, I passed the case with the Three Teardrops. One of them had slipped out of place. So I got the key back from Angelo and unlocked the case. I saw that the stones were not the real ones. The real sapphires have marks on them— very faint lines."

"Yes, I noticed that at the museum," Barbie told her. "I wondered about it."

"No one knows exactly why the lines are there. But that's how we know they're the real ones," Gina explained. "But anyway, I had to act fast. I told our security guard no one was to leave without having his or her bags searched. The museum was closed to visitors today, so only my staff was there."

"Well, if the gems weren't found, maybe they're still at the museum," Barbie suggested.

"Yes, unless . . . Let me look at your gown, Barbie," Gina said. "Maybe Toni somehow put the real ones on your dress by mistake."

They unzipped the white bag. Gina took one look and then shook her head. "No. These are imitation sapphires, all right. Angelo told me I shouldn't have taken them out. I should have listened to him!" She put her head in her hands.

Barbie touched Gina's arm. "Tell me exactly what happened after I left. When did the set of imitation sapphires show up?"

Gina looked up and sighed. "Just after you left," she replied. "I was at the door waiting for another delivery when the messenger came."

"And what did you do with the package?" Barbie asked.

"I gave it to Angelo," the director answered. "I asked him to bring it to Toni so she could finish your dress."

"At that point, did Angelo still have the key to the case?" Barbie asked.

Gina nodded. Then she looked alarmed. "But you don't think . . . not Angelo! He's the person I trust most in the world! Could he have switched the real sapphires with imitations?"

"Let's not jump to conclusions," Barbie cautioned. "At this point, we don't know what happened. But I promise, Gina, I'll help you figure it out. Meanwhile, shouldn't you call the police?"

"Museum security has already called them. The ball begins in less than two hours. So I asked our head of security to handle the problem," Gina replied. "Well, you had better get ready. And so should I, even though I don't feel like going to a party."

Barbie patted Gina's shoulder. "Don't worry. We'll get the jewels back," she promised. She just didn't know how.

Barbie showered. She curled and pinned her hair. Then she sprinkled powder on it as people had done long ago. She added a blue ribbon and put on her makeup. Then she very carefully stepped into the beautiful ball gown. The whole time, her mind was on the puzzling mystery.

Barbie liked Angelo. But she remembered how angry he had looked when Gina had spoken sharply to him. He could be angry because he hadn't been chosen for museum director.

But was Angelo angry enough to have stolen the real sapphires and put fake ones in their place? And for what reason? To make Gina look bad? To make her lose her job?

"Or," Barbie hated even to think it, "maybe Gina wasn't telling the truth. She herself could have made the switch. After all, she was the director. And she had the key to the case."

Barbie looked at the clock. She put lipstick and a comb into the jeweled purse. She was surprised to see something stuffed inside.

She pulled out a slip of paper. It was

written in Italian, so she couldn't read it. But it looked like a **receipt** from a store. Barbie could see that it was dated July 14. She checked the date on her calendar. It said the fifteenth.

"The fourteenth was yesterday," Barbie said out loud. "Something was delivered to the museum yesterday. But there were probably lots of deliveries because of the ball."

Her eyes looked over the paper. A word seemed to leap out at her. *Zaffiri!*

Barbie remembered what Angelo had told her. "*Zaffiri* is the Italian word for sapphires!" she exclaimed. "That's odd. Gina said the first set of imitation sapphires never arrived yesterday. But according to this, she was wrong. One set *did* come yesterday. And the second set came today." She looked down at the gown she was wearing.

"One set was put onto my dress. And the second set must have been placed in the display case. That hid the fact that the real ones had been taken."

She looked again at the slip of paper in her hand. "Someone at the museum must have signed this receipt. And whoever signed must be the one behind the switch!"

On the **signature** line was a handwriting she couldn't quite make out. But the first two letters in the first name were very clear.

"*A-n,*" she whispered. "Angelo!"

Chapter Five

Soon after, Barbie was riding in a gondola to the ball.

"Unfortunately, it does look as if Angelo's our man," thought Barbie. The gondola glided slowly through the canal. "He must have signed for the fake gems yesterday and kept them out of sight. Then he waited for a good time to make the switch. And with all the fuss about the magazine photographer, today was perfect."

She stepped out of the gondola in front of the museum. "It's just so hard to believe. There must be more to the story," she thought, frowning.

Lively orchestra music drifted from the museum as Barbie walked up the marble steps. Inside, the mansion sparkled with light from the chandeliers overhead. Elegantly dressed men and women greeted one another. Everyone was wearing a mask.

A short woman in a dark red, velvet gown came over to Barbie. A scarf of red ostrich feathers was draped over her shoulders. Her face was covered with a red-feathered mask. But Barbie recognized the flashing brown eyes as Gina's.

Tonight those eyes looked worried as they gazed across the room to where Angelo stood. He wore a checkered outfit and a three-pointed hat. It was the costume of the famous Italian clowns called *harlequins.* He wore a matching mask over his face. When he lifted his mask, Barbie noticed his mouth looked angry.

"Angelo is furious," Gina told Barbie. "He

says that I'm treating him like a criminal because I had his things searched with everyone else's. What else could I do? Now he says he might quit."

"I found something you should see," Barbie stated. She took the receipt out of her purse.

A man dressed as a sailor approached Gina for a dance.

"He has given a lot of money to the museum," the director whispered to Barbie. "I had better go."

"Take this," Barbie finished. She slipped the receipt into Gina's hand.

Gina nodded as she glided onto the dance floor. "Your speech is at ten o'clock," she told Barbie. "I'll come get you."

Angelo soon found Barbie and invited her to dance. The two circled around the crowded dance floor. Angelo's talk was polite. But he seemed to be thinking of other things. He didn't say anything about the missing jewels. At one end of the room, the display of gowns had been set up. Barbie could

see that the display of dresses was creating a lot of excitement. Groups of people moved from one gown to another. They were talking and admiring them, pointing out different parts.

When the music ended, Barbie went over to the entrance. She signed her name in the fancy, blue guest book. Then she did a double take. The signature a few lines above hers looked familiar. Barbie saw that the name began with *A-n*. She realized the handwriting looked just like the one on the receipt!

But this time Barbie could read the whole signature.

Antonetta Mazzoli.

So Angelo was *not* the person who had signed the receipt! But who was Antonetta Mazzoli?

A couple danced by. The woman was wearing a brown silk gown with a ruffled hem. Barbie remembered the gown Toni had been sewing in the workroom. Hadn't Gina said Toni was working on the gown she would wear tonight? The woman wore a gold mask. But her bright blue eyes stood out as she talked with her partner. Barbie smiled. It was Toni, all right.

Toni kept glancing at her watch. It was close to ten o'clock. In a few minutes it would be time for Barbie to give her speech.

Toni was dancing across the room now. Barbie could see the woman's reflection in the darkened windows. But the bottom of her dress looked strange. The smooth material was bunched and lumpy. Toni was a skilled seamstress. Why would she do such sloppy work on her own dress?

Suddenly a thought hit Barbie. Of course! She began to push her way through the crowd of masked dancers. "Toni!" she cried. "Wait!"

But when she reached the other side of the room, she found she was too late. Toni was gone!

Chapter Six

Following a hunch, Barbie headed for the back of the museum. As she walked, the music became fainter and fainter. The rooms were dark and silent. Barbie made her way to the workroom where she had tried on her gown earlier that day.

Barbie went inside. In the moonlight, she saw a woman standing perfectly still.

"Hello?" Barbie called. "Toni?"

She stepped closer. The woman didn't move.

Then Barbie covered up a laugh. It was the dressmaker's dummy!

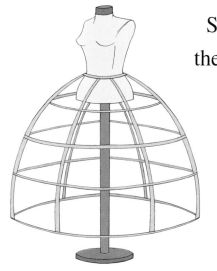

She slowly looked around the room, but no one was there. Through the glass doors, Barbie saw a movement outside.

She quietly opened a door and slipped out into the night air.

Barbie saw Toni standing in the garden. The masked woman was holding up an object that glinted in the moonlight like steel. Sharp steel.

Barbie hid behind a tree and watched.

Toni bent down and picked up the hem of her dress. And now Barbie could see that the sharp object was a pair of scissors.

With a quick motion, the bottom of the gown was cut. Toni caught three objects as they tumbled out. One, two, three.

Barbie was sure she knew what they were. "The Three Teardrops!" she whispered to herself.

"And I'll bet Toni is a nickname for Antonetta—Antonetta Mazzoli!"

While Barbie's mind raced to put everything together, Toni switched on a small flashlight. She studied the sapphires carefully, one by one.

"Toni must have signed for the first set of imitation sapphires yesterday. But she didn't tell Gina." Barbie thought back to the sparkling objects in Toni's sewing basket. "She must have hidden them there. Then I left to change out of the gown. And Toni switched the fakes with the real jewels from the case. She gave that first set of fakes to Angelo to put back in the case. He was probably in such a hurry to return the jewels that he never noticed the difference. Later, when the second set arrived, Toni put those on my gown."

Then Barbie watched as Toni did something even stranger. She shined her flashlight on the old bricks on the ground. She moved the light around and around, kneeling down to see better.

Then she gave a cry of joy.

Barbie had no idea what Toni was doing. But something told her to stay hidden.

From the stack of workers' tools, Toni grabbed a small shovel. She dug and poked around the bricks. Then she dropped the shovel and began tugging at the bricks with her fingers.

Finally Toni pulled three bricks free, one after another. She reached down and—

Gina's voice rang out in the workroom. "Barbie! Where are you? I have to ask you about the receipt you gave me!"

The museum director walked into the garden. Puzzled, she looked at Toni. "What in the world is going on?" she demanded.

Barbie stepped out of the shadows. "I can answer part of that question," she replied.

"And I will answer the rest," Toni added.

The glass door opened again, and Angelo hurried outside. "Everyone's looking for you,

Barbie. It's time for your speech." Then he, too, looked puzzled. "What's everyone doing out here?"

Finally Toni removed her mask. She pushed strands of blond hair out of her face. On the ground next to her lay the Three Teardrops. And next to them was an antique metal box, caked with dirt.

Angelo saw the jewels on the ground. With a cry, he rushed to scoop them up. Then he pointed a shaking finger at Toni. "You're the thief! You stole the Three Teardrops!"

Toni's voice was calm. "I didn't steal the Three Teardrops. I replaced fakes with other fakes. The *real* jewels are in this old box. They were hidden here by the duchess herself two hundred years ago."

"What?" exclaimed Gina.

"You're talking nonsense!" stated Angelo.

"Maybe we should go back into the workroom," suggested Barbie. "I think we all could use a little help understanding what happened."

Once inside, Gina carefully opened the metal box. There was a loud gasp as everyone saw what was inside.

Under layers of straw, still wrapped in tattered paper, were three amazing blue jewels. Barbie saw that their color was much closer to the drawing she had seen in the Venice history book. They seemed to bathe the room in blue light.

Gina broke the stunned silence. "But Toni, how did you know they were there?"

"Because Duchess Venezia is my ancestor," Toni replied. "My grandmother told me her story many times. She also told me a family rumor: the sapphires passed down through generations were not real! But they had certain marks that were clues to where the real ones were hidden."

Toni took the museum's gems from Angelo. "The marks are the Roman numerals one, two,

and three." She pointed to the three bricks she had pulled up. "See? Those bricks have the same marks. They were grouped together, and the box was underneath the bricks."

Toni smiled. "The bench that once stood on those bricks was so important to Duchess Venezia's story. I guessed that she would have hidden them close by."

"But why did she hide them in the first place?" asked Angelo.

"To protect them," Toni replied. "When she was a very old woman, Venice was invaded. The duchess was afraid enemy troops would steal them. She had imitation gems made and marked them. Then she buried the real ones. Sadly, by the time the danger passed, she was dead. She never had a chance to tell anyone where the hiding place was."

Gina held up the receipt. "So you planned this whole thing, Toni? You didn't even tell me when the first set of copies came in yesterday."

"I didn't plan that part," Toni confessed. "I was going to tell you that the first copies had come. Then you and Barbie came in for the fitting. And my mouth was full of pins! I had the copies in my sewing basket. I must have stuffed the receipt in whatever I was working on at the time. Then you decided to use the 'real' sapphires from the museum case on Barbie's dress. Immediately I saw a chance to switch them with the copies in my basket. I only wanted to study the marks, so I could find the hiding place. I knew it had to be somewhere in the garden. And with workers digging tomorrow, the treasured sapphires could have been damaged or lost forever."

Barbie spoke up. "And when Gina discovered the switch, she ordered everyone's things searched. So you sewed the museum copies into your hem."

Toni nodded. Gently she touched the gleaming jewels in the box. "I only wanted the truth to be known so the museum would have the real sapphires. I don't pretend to own these beautiful jewels. They keep the memory of the duchess alive and should remain here forever."

"Why didn't you tell me all of this sooner?" Gina asked. "I would have let you look at the markings on the other gems. And all of us at the museum would have helped you search for the real sapphires."

Toni shook her head. "I didn't know if my grandmother's story was true or not," she replied. "How could I tell experts that their 'treasured sapphires' were fakes? If the story wasn't true, I would have created a fuss over nothing."

"Well, you frightened us. But we owe you a thank-you," said Gina. "And tomorrow I will tell the museum board exactly what has happened. Won't they be surprised! And I will ask for a grand, new case worthy of the *real* Three Teardrops. As for the marked copies that we've thought were real for so long—"

Barbie interrupted. "I have an idea about those. Could Toni make another switch? Could she replace the copies on my dress with the museum copies marked with numerals? Then I can tell the *whole* story of the Three Teardrops when I take the gowns on tour. It will add even more interest."

"And sell even more tickets!" Gina cried.

Tears of happiness shone in Toni's blue eyes. Her likeness to Duchess Venezia was now very clear to Barbie.

"I will switch them right after the ball," Toni promised.

Gina looked at her watch. "Now you have a speech to give, Barbie."

"And a European tour to begin!" Barbie exclaimed. "One that couldn't be off to a more exciting start!"

My scrapbook of Venice, Italy

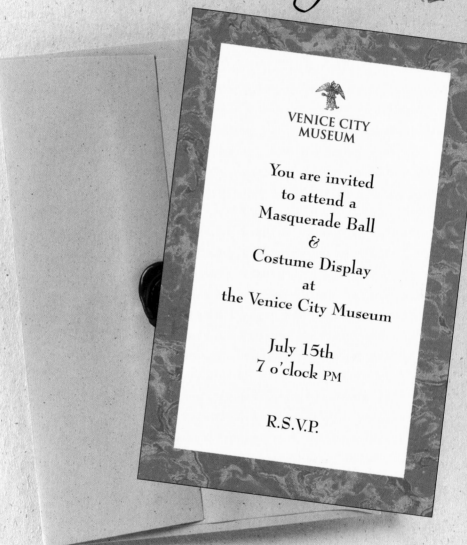

VENICE CITY MUSEUM

You are invited
to attend a
Masquerade Ball
&
Costume Display
at
the Venice City Museum

July 15th
7 o'clock PM

R.S.V.P.

Wow! What a fabulous trip! I just loved Venice! Besides solving an exciting mystery, I had the chance to visit a beautiful, old city. Venice is called a lagoon city because it's really a series of tiny islands connected by over 400 bridges. Beautiful buildings line the canals—it was hard to stop taking pictures. I can't wait to go back!

Petals from a rose in my hotel room.

Here's the balcony off my hotel room. The wood shutters and flowerpots are so charming! I had a wonderful view of the city.

© Kim Riordan

This is St. Mark's square—it's considered the center of Venice.

© Kathlene Persoff

This is a map of Venice from my guidebook. Narrow waterways called canals run between the islands.

Venice

© MapQuest.com

It was fun taking a gondola from place to place.
Its driver is called a gondolier (gon-duh-LEAR). He stands
in the back of the boat to row it. He uses a single oar
as a pole to push the boat along.

I saw these red-and-white poles all over Venice. Gondoliers tie their boats to them.

Biglietto 24 ore
24 Stunden Fahrkarte
24 hours ticket
Billet 24 heures

Actv

N° 63919 Z

8000

Lire

I love traveling in style! Just look at this gondola I took to the museum.

There are almost no cars in Venice. But with waterbuses, gondolas, gondola-ferries, and water taxis, Venice still has its share of traffic jams!

St. Mark's Basilica (buh-SI-li-kuh) was one of my favorite places to visit. This beautiful church was built over 1000 years ago.

BASILICA DI S. MARCO

I loved the majestic Doges' (DOH-jis) Palace. With its amazing architecture, it's easy to see why dukes used to live and rule here.

Here's the market where I bought gifts for my sisters. The shopkeepers were so friendly.

This is Italian currency, which is called Lire (LEAR-uh).

The Rialto (ree-AL-toh) Bridge is one of only three bridges that cross the Grand Canal. Angelo and I sailed under it when I first arrived in Venice.

A master mask maker gave
this feather to me while
I was in his mask shop.

Gina said that in the 1600s, there
were more than 15,000 gondolas
jamming the canals. Today, only
about 350 exist, mainly for
visitors like me!

One night after dinner, we took a
water taxi along the Grand Canal. The sunset was
breathtaking. The taxi driver explained that the Grand Canal
is 2 1/4 miles long. It winds through the heart of Venice.
More than 200 beautiful palaces line its banks.

I saw these stunning masks in a shop window. Venice is famous for its tradition of masked balls. I'm lucky to have attended one—and to have worn such a beautiful dress. Here is a sketch of the dress I wore.

© A. Auerbach

Venice is also famous for its fine and delicate lace.